Tawatawa 1st XV

POUWHENUA STATUE
HAPPY VALLEY
TAWATAWA RESERVE
HAPPY VALLEY PARK
TAWATAWA 1st XV GROUNDS
CITY TO SEA WALKWAY
MURCHISON STREET

Tawatawa 1st XV

Written by Hannah Abrams • Illustrated by Joni Dawson

To all the dogs of Tawatawa,
past, present and future.

TAWATAWA
RESERVE

Long before sun-up, they're out on the hill,
their breath is all steamy, their paws feel the chill.
First come the greetings, 'Kia ora, old chums!'
Then lots of loud barks and the sniffing of bums.
They've all practised hard, they won't be outsmarted,
now the team is all here, and the game can get started!

Off they all trot with a bustle and bark,
following the path that winds down to the park.
With their tails in the air, they're all happy and keen.
All kinds of dogs, both chubby and lean.
Snaking their way down the slippery track,
Rhodie's out front with Meeloo at back.

Onto the field they run into position,
the coach has a plan, but it might be a mission.
All that he wants is good fun and fair play,
and a bunch of tired dogs at the end of the day.
Then the whistle is blown, the game has begun,
the ball is in play and they're ready for fun!

Down comes the ball, bouncing straight to Meeloo,
she eyes up the field and she knows what to do.
Down past the ten-metre line she runs through,
dodging a tackle, she makes the twenty-two.
Through legs, around players, going over and under,
it looks like a try until . . . whoops, there's a blunder!

It rolls over to Socks who jumps at the chance.
This halfback's a ball hog – look at her dance!
A step to the left and then one to the right,
then she's off down the field, not a player in sight.
Her speed and her footwork are meant to impress,
but how long will she hog it? It's anyone's guess!

Now the props power forward, stopping Socks on the spot.
Mickey and Bailey give it all that they've got.
They bulldoze and shove, there's no way that they'll yield,
then they bang into Midge . . . the ball rolls off the field.
There's a tight roly-poly and then a quick throw,
and a high snatch by Ollie, who runs tight and low.

Sam and Takarua stand like a wall;
Takarua barks loudly, and they both grab the ball.
But they're ambushed by Dipper and Echo, the locks,
and on pile old Piper and Tui and Socks.
But out of this scuffle the two flankers push,
till they crash into Boston . . . and the ball's in the bush!

While Steve pulls the ball from the gorse with his rake,
the team grab a quick wharepaku break.
Such relief when they're done, and they've had a good leak,
but now half the team have gone down to the creek!
So the coach calls a lineout and yells at the pack:
'We're ready to throw in, so get yourselves back.'

From the lineout the locks are now showing their skills,
using the leaps that they've practised in drills.
Dipper and Echo, that dynamic pair,
with ease and precision they soar through the air.
Snatching the ball, they take off at pace,
and run down the pitch with such ease and such grace.

Hang on, did someone say, ‘Time for a snack?’
Was it that porky one there at the back?
Refuelling the troops is important, it’s true,
but not when they’re heading towards a breakthrough!
Boston the hooker’s not one to miss out,
not when he’s got that super-sized snout!

Now Midge and Meeloo get them all back on track.
And Socks motors in, she's a stunning halfback!
Midge gets the ball, don't be fooled by her size —
nothing escapes her tiny brown eyes.

Piper, the centre, is straight on the job.
She tackles down Midge, gives the ball a quick lob.
With that chip and run, it's anyone's guess,
could this be the chance that they need? That's a 'Yes!'
Then one lucky bounce, and just on full time,
the whistle sounds out as she crosses that line!

Now the game's over, it's time to cool down.
They roll in the mud and their coats turn to brown.
They run to their owners, who rub them all down,
then it's into the cars and away back to town.
They'll be back next Saturday, scrubbed up and keen,
the dogs from the Tawatawa 1st XV!

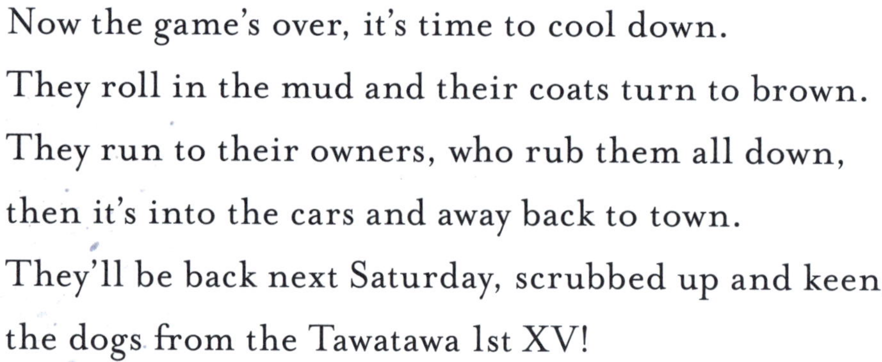

With special thanks to Stephen, Miriam and Bill.

Published in 2023 by David Bateman Ltd,
Unit 2/5 Workspace Drive, Hobsonville,
Auckland 0618, New Zealand
www.batemanbooks.co.nz
ISBN: 978-1-77689-087-3

A catalogue record for this book is available
from the National Library of New Zealand.

Book design: Alice Bell
Printed in China by Toppan Leefung Printing Ltd